A Pet's Life

Dogs

Anita Ganeri

Heinemann Library
Chicago, Illinois

www.heinemannraintree.com
Visit our website to find out
more information about
Heinemann-Raintree books.

To order:
☎ Phone 888-454-2279
💻 Visit www.heinemannraintree.com
to browse our catalog and order online.

© 2009 Heinemann Library
an imprint of Capstone Global Library, LLC
Chicago, Illinois

Customer Service: 888-454-2279

Visit our website at www.heinemannraintree.com

Printed and bound by South China Printing Company Ltd

13 12 11 10 09
10 9 8 7 6 5 4 3 2

Library of Congress Cataloging-in-Publication Data
New edition ISBN: 978 14329 3390 6 (hardcover) – 978
14329 3397 5 (paperback)
The Library of Congress has cataloged the first edition as
follows:
Ganeri, Anita, 1961-
  Dogs / Anita Ganeri.
     v. cm. -- (A pet's life) (Heinemann first library)
Includes bibliographical references and index.
Contents: What is a dog? -- Dog babies -- Your pet dog --
Choosing your
dog -- Things to get ready -- Welcome home -- Feeding time
-- Playing
with your dog -- Training your dog -- Growing up -- A
healthy dog -- Old
age.
  ISBN 1-4034-3994-X (hardcover) -- ISBN 1-4034-4270-3
(pbk.)
  1. Dogs--Juvenile literature. [1. Dogs. 2. Pets.] I. Title. II.
Series.
  SF426.5.G36 2003
  636.7--dc21

508 274 4   2002151592

Acknowledgments
The author and publishers are grateful to the following for
permission to reproduce copyright material:
Alamy p. **22** (© TNT MAGAZINE); Ardea pp. **7**, **14** (© John
Daniels); © Capstone Global Library Ltd. pp. **8** (Mark Farrell),
19, **25** (Trevor Clifford), **5**, **12**, **13**, **16**, **17**, **20**, **24**, **27** (Tudor
Photography); Getty Images p. **23** (The Image Bank/LWA);
Masterfile p. **15** (Alison Barnes Martin); Photolibrary p. **18**
(Juniors Bildarchiv); RSPCA p. **26** (Colin Seddon); Shutterstock
p. **4** (© Eric Isselée); Warren Photographic pp. **6**, **9**, **11**, **21** (Jane
Burton), **10**.

Cover photograph reproduced with permission of Photolibrary
(Juniors Bildarchiv).

The publishers would like to thank Judy Tuma for her
invaluable assistance in the preparation of this book.

Contents

Some words are shown in bold, **like this**. You can find out what they mean by looking in the Glossary.

What Do Dogs Look Like?

Dogs come in many different sizes, shapes, and colors. They can have long or short hair. Most dogs have tails that they can wag. Dogs make wonderful pets.

Dogs can be very big, or very tiny!

This picture shows the different parts of a dog's body. You can see what each part is used for.

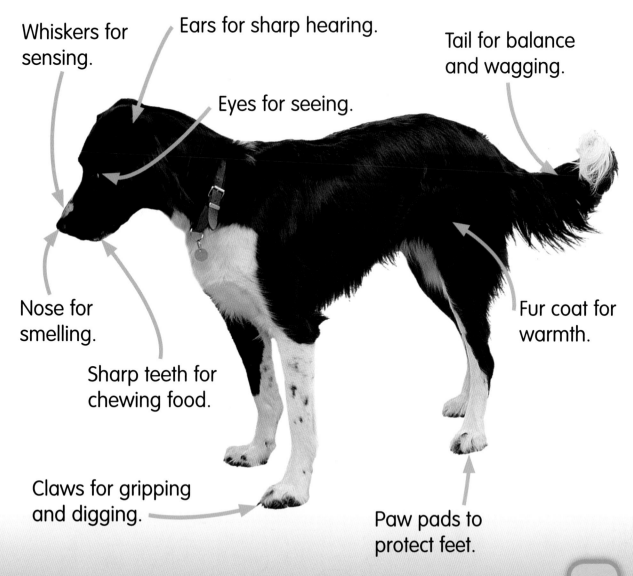

Whiskers for sensing.

Ears for sharp hearing.

Tail for balance and wagging.

Eyes for seeing.

Nose for smelling.

Fur coat for warmth.

Sharp teeth for chewing food.

Claws for gripping and digging.

Paw pads to protect feet.

Dog Babies

Baby dogs are called puppies. Small dogs may have up to six puppies in a **litter**. Large dogs may have as many as twelve puppies.

A mother dog feeds her puppies with milk.

The **veterinarian** will decide when your puppy should have **vaccinations** to stop it becoming sick.

Puppies must stay with their mother until they are at least eight weeks old. Then they are old enough to be chosen as pets.

Choosing Your Dog

Animal shelters have many dogs and puppies that need loving homes. You might want to pick an older dog instead of a puppy.

The people at the shelter will help you to pick the right dog for you.

Choose a lively, happy dog with a clean, shiny coat, clean ears, and bright eyes. These are signs that the dog is healthy.

Look for an active dog that is happy to see you.

Growing Up

As your puppy grows up, you will get to know it very well. When it wags its tail fast, it means that it is happy to see you.

Bowing like this means that your dog wants to play.

Dogs and puppies are fun, but they need a lot of care. You will need to look after your dog for the whole of its life. This could be from 10 to 18 years.

If you look after your dog, you will quickly become its best friend.

Things to Get Ready

Get everything ready before you bring your new pet home. Your dog needs a bed with a washable blanket. It needs bowls for food and water, and toys to play with.

A chew-proof dog bed is best for your pet.

Your dog must wear a **collar** and tag. The tag should have your name and address on it, in case your pet gets lost. Always put your dog on a **leash** when you take it for a walk.

You should put your dog's name on the tag, too.

Welcome Home

Put your dog's bed in the room where you want it to sleep at night. For the first few nights you may have to place your dog in its new bed.

A dog might feel lonely on its first night in its new home.

Cats and dogs can get along well once they get to know each other.

If you have other pets, introduce them slowly to your dog. Don't leave them alone together right away. After a while, they should become good friends.

Feeding Time

Adult dogs need one or two meals a day. Puppies need three or four smaller meals. You can feed your dog dry or canned dog food. Dry dog food is better for its teeth.

Feed your dog or puppy at the same time every day.

Rawhide bones are good for cleaning your dog's teeth.

Make sure that your dog always has fresh water to drink. You can sometimes give your dog a biscuit or a rawhide bone as a treat.

Playing With Your Dog

Dogs like toys that they can chew. You can buy dog toys from a pet shop. Buy well-made toys that are too big for your dog to swallow.

Dogs love to play games of fetch and catch with balls and frisbees.

Dogs need lots of exercise to stay healthy.

You should take your dog for a walk twice a day. Always clean up the waste **your dog leaves on the ground**. Ask an adult to show you how to stay clean when you do this.

Training Your Dog

All dogs and puppies need to be trained. You should teach your dog to come when you call its name, and to sit down and stay when you tell it to.

You can train your dog at home or take it to a dog training class.

Praise your puppy when it uses the newspaper. Never scold it if it makes a mistake.

Puppies need to learn to go to the bathroom outside. Put some newspaper down for your puppy to use. Every day, slowly move the newspaper closer to the door.

Family Pet

If you cannot take your dog on vacation, you might be able to leave it with a friend or neighbor. Otherwise you can put your dog in a **boarding kennel**.

Boarding kennels are like hotels for dogs.

Your dog can become your family's best friend!

Older dogs become part of the family. Your dog will enjoy taking walks, going on vacation, and spending time with you.

A Healthy Dog

If you take care of your dog, it should stay fit and healthy. Take your dog to the **veterinarian** if you are worried about it.

If your dog does not want to eat or play, it might be sick. Take it to the veterinarian to find out what is wrong.

The veterinarian can also clip your dog's nails so that it doesn't scratch itself.

You should take your dog to the veterinarian once a year. The veterinarian will check your dog all over and give it **vaccinations** to keep it healthy.

Old Age

As your dog gets older, it might not be able to see or hear as well as before. But it will still enjoy doing things with you. An older dog should be given senior dog food.

An older dog may want to sleep more often.

Your older dog will not have as much energy as a puppy. It still needs to be given food and water and taken for walks every day.

Caring for your dog will help you learn how to treat animals properly.

Useful Tips

- If you want to pick up your puppy, put one hand under its chest and the other hand under its bottom.

- **Groom** your dog every day to keep its coat clean and shiny, and to get out any old hair.

- Ask your **veterinarian** what you should do stop your dog getting fleas and worms.

- If you cannot have a dog at home, you and your family could visit the dogs at an **animal shelter**.

- Do not let your puppy outside before it has its first **vaccinations**. It might catch a **disease** from another dog.

- Dogs like company. It is not fair to get a dog and leave it at home alone for a long time each day.

Fact File

- All pet dogs are related to wolves. Wolves were probably first kept as pets about 12,000 to 15,000 years ago.

- In ancient China, people thought that dogs scared off evil spirits.

- There are about 200 million pet dogs around the world.

- The heaviest **breeds** of pet dog are the St. Bernard and the mastiff. The tallest dog breed is the Irish wolfhound.

- The oldest pet dog known was an Australian cattle-dog called Bluey. He died in 1939, at the age of 29.

- Dogs have an amazing sense of smell. A dog can smell things more than a hundred times better than you can.

Glossary

animal shelter place where lost or unwanted animals are looked after and found new homes

boarding kennels place where you can leave your dog when you go on vacation

breed kind or type of animal

disease sickness

groom brush or clean your dog

leash line for holding an animal

litter puppies born at the same time

related being part of the same family

vaccination medicine that is given by a veterinarian to stop dogs catching diseases

veterinarian specially trained animal doctor

More Books to Read

An older reader can help you with these books.

Calmenson, Stephanie, and Jan Ormerod. *May I Pet Your Dog?: The How-to Guide for Kids Meeting Dogs (and Dogs Meeting Kids)*. New York: Clarion Books, 2007.

Boyer Binns, Tristan. *Keeping Pets: Dogs*. Chicago, IL: Heinemann Library, 2004.

Evans, Mark. *Puppy (ASPCA Pet Guides for Kids)*. Minneapolis, MN.: Turtleback Books, 2002.

Kim, Bryan. *How to Look After Your Pet: Puppy Care*. New York: Dorling Kindersley Publishing Inc., 2004.

Roca, Nuria and Rosa M. Curto. *Let's Take Care of Our New Dog*. New York: Barron's Educational Series, 2006.

Index